For Phoebe — RH
For my mother — SW

First published in Great Britain in 2003 by Bloomsbury Publishing Plc
38 Soho Square, London, W1D 3HB

Text copyright © Richard Hamilton 2003
Illustrations copyright © Sophy Williams 2003
The moral right of the author and illustrator has been asserted

A CIP catalogue record of this book is available from the British Library
ISBN 0 7475 6101 X

Designed by Sarah Hodder

Printed in Hong Kong/China

3 5 7 9 10 8 6 4 2

# Polly's Picnic

by Richard Hamilton

illustrated by Sophy Williams

BLOOMSBURY
CHILDREN'S
BOOKS

When the sun shone brightly
in the clear blue sky and the
summer birds darted through the air —

Polly went for a picnic, down by the river.

She lay in the sun, popped open some crisps
and lazily started to dream ...

Then —

Quack-Quack!
Attack!

Some ducks stole her snack
and gobbled it up
in midstream!

Polly opened up her sandwich box
and found beside her — Mr Fox.

"Go on," she said, "have one."
He did ... and two ... and three ... and four.
He ate until there were no more.

She poured some milk into a cup
and — in a flash — two cats purred up.

Polly wasn't pleased but she could see
that they were hungrier than she.

"Have a sip," said Polly.
"It's awfully hot."
But those greedy cats
drank every drop!

"Hey!" cried Polly. "I'm thirsty too —
I didn't bring that milk for you."

Then, in her basket, she found a pear,
and suddenly, a horse was there.

"Have a bite," said Polly. "One bite. NO MORE."
But he ate it all — even the core!

Polly gasped,
　　Polly growled.
　　　　Polly very nearly howled!

"Can I have some?" asked a goat,
emerging from the undergrowth.

Polly snapped, "The basket's empty."
The goat replied, "That looks like plenty."

He opened his mouth,
he licked his lips,
he chewed the basket into bits!

When the sun shone brightly
in the clear blue sky
and the summer birds
darted through the air —

Polly cried:
"It's just not fair.
I gave you my food
and drink for free

and now there's nothing left for me.
No one said thank you,
no one said please!
You've ruined my picnic under the trees!"

A swan gliding past, heard her complain
and said to the ducks,
"You should be ashamed —
Polly's upset
because of your greed.
You must put this right
with all possible speed."

So the ducks
asked the fox,

and the fox
asked the cats.

The cats asked the horse,
the horse asked the goat.

Who's been greedy?
Who's been rude?
Who has stolen
Polly's food?

Jumping on the horse's back
they galloped smartly up the track.

"There's Polly's house," the two cats cried.
They found the door and burst inside.

Then they measured, mixed and baked biscuits, sandwiches, sausages, cakes.

Back to the river they carried the food
on heads and tails, in paws and hooves.

There they found Polly, looking sad.
"We're sorry," they said. "We've been terribly bad."

Together they had a picnic tea
and everybody shared
with everybody.

"Friends," said Polly, "I am no longer sad.
That's the best picnic tea I've ever had.

Thank you!"